W9-BIY-295

I Have A New Friend

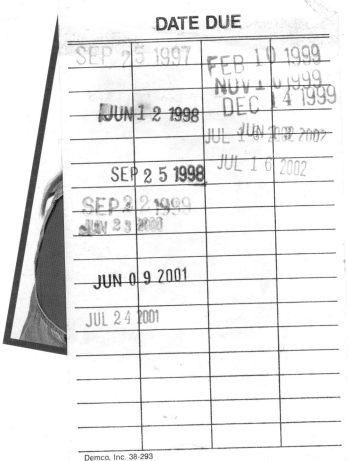

Kathleen Allan-Meyer

with
Photo Illustrations by
Mike Spinelli

BARRON'S

Dedicated To Ro Logrippo

All inquiries should be addressed to:
Barron's Educational Series, Inc.
250 Wireless Boulevard
Hauppauge, New York 11788

International Standard Book No. 0-8120-9408-5 (paperback)
International Standard Book No. 0-8120-6532-8 (hardcover)

Library of Congress Catalog Card No. 95-5803

Library of Congress Cataloging-In-Publication Data

Allan-Meyer, Kathleen.
    I have a new friend / by Kathleen Allan-Meyer ; with photo
illustrations by Mike Spinelli.
        p.   cm.
    Summary: Lisa writes a letter to her grandmother telling all about
her new Japanese friend at nursery school.
    ISBN 0-8120-6532-8. — ISBN 0-8120-9408-5 (pbk.)
    [1. Friendship—Fiction. 2. Nursery schools—Fiction.
3. Schools—Fiction. 4. Japan—Fiction. 5. Letters—Fiction.]
I. Spinelli, Mike, ill.   II. Title.
PZ7. M5717114lah   1995
[E]—dc20

95-5803
CIP
AC

Printed in Hong Kong
5678   9955   987654321

Dear Grandma,

I have a new friend. Her name is Saki.

Saki is Japanese. And she just came to America. We go to the same school.

We like to play in the Home Center best.

Sometimes I am the mother and wear the apron. Sometimes Saki pretends she is the mother. Then SHE wheels the carriage.

We like to paint pictures next to each other.

We like the same colors and we share them.

Playing in the rhythm band together is fun. I always choose the triangle, and Saki likes the bells. Sometimes we change.

Then we march around and around to "Yankee Doodle." We don't speak English or Japanese. We just laugh.

Sometimes after school our moms take us to the park. Playing train on the slide is the most fun.

Then we get very hungry. We sit on the grass and eat peanut butter and jelly sandwiches. I don't think Saki ever ate them before. But she really likes them.

One day Saki's mother asked if I could come over to their house for lunch. Mom said that it would be OK.

We had Japanese food. Saki's mom called it teriyaki. You eat it with chopsticks. People in Japan use them instead of knives and forks.

The food kept falling off my chopsticks. I was getting very hungry.

Then Saki's mother gave me a fork. I am learning to like teriyaki. But I still need a fork.

A few days later Saki came to play. When she went into our house, she took off her shoes. Mom said that is what Japanese people do.

I thought that was a fun thing to do. Now, whenever I go to Saki's house, I take my shoes off, too.

At my house, we had spaghetti and meatballs for lunch. I started to sing a funny song, "On Top of Spaghetti." We learned it in school.

Then we pretended the spaghetti were worms. Saki ate up ALL of her worms.

When it was almost time for Halloween, I asked Saki what she was going to be. She didn't understand. Her Mom said that they don't have Halloween in Japan.

I showed Saki a picture about Halloween in my book.

Then I dressed up in my queen costume and walked around with my trick-or-treat bag.

I wanted Saki to celebrate Halloween, too.
Mom said, "Maybe Saki would like to use
your costume from last year. You're too big
to wear it anymore."

Saki liked that idea and I helped her get dressed.

We had fun at our Halloween party. Saki looked so pretty as a fairy princess—and I was the beautiful queen.

Guess what, Grandma? All the food was orange!

They don't have Valentine's Day in Japan either. So I thought I better tell Saki about that, too.

A few days before our valentine party at school I showed Saki how to make valentines with paper doilies and heart stickers.

I like Saki and I made her a special
valentine. She got lots of valentines from our
class mailbox, but she liked mine best of all.
I could tell.

One day Saki invited me to a Japanese celebration—Hina Matsuri (Hee-na-matsree). That means Girls' Day. It's always on March 3.

Everything looked so pretty in her living room on Saki's special day.

There were beautiful dolls in kimonos and shiny little black furniture on bright red steps.

And guess what, Grandma? Saki was dressed in a kimono, too. Then Saki's mom dressed me up in a kimono. We looked so pretty!

I wished I was Japanese so I could celebrate Girls' Day at my house every year.

Last week when we sat in our circle at school, our teacher told us there are many different kinds of people living in our city.

Each of us, she said, is the same in lots of ways just like Saki and me.

And each of us is different in many ways just like Saki and me.

But she said we are all special. And the best way to get along is to learn more about each other.

I think that's what Saki and I are doing, Grandma. And it's fun!

Love,

LISA

HINA MATSURI

Japan is a land of many beautiful festivals. The Japanese word for festival is "matsuri."

A favorite festival for girls is Hina Matsuri, held each year on March 3. Hina is the Japanese name for a special set of dolls that families with girls put on display on Hina Matsuri. These dolls are not meant to play with. They are very valuable and are often handed down from mother to daughter.

A series of shelves, looking much like steps, is set up. These steps are covered with red cloth.

Hina dolls wear beautiful clothes that are called kimonos. These dolls wear court costumes used 1,000 years ago.

On the top shelf, in the place of honor, are the emperor and the empress. The emperor has a sword and staff. The empress has a fan.

Two floor lamps with paper shades are called bon bories. Below them are members of the royal court. First, there are three ladies in waiting. They serve tea, Japanese wine, and food. Then there are five musicians. One of them is the singer. The others play the flute and the hand drum. There are two officials and finally, three guardsmen.

There are also diamond-shaped rice cakes, miniature household articles, and furniture.

After the festival, everything is carefully packed away until the next year.

During Hina Matsuri, the Japanese wish for all the little girls to grow up healthy and pretty.

WORDS TO KNOW

chopsticks—the long, thin wooden sticks that Japanese people use for eating Japanese food.

teriyaki—a Japanese main course made with any meat or fish that is broiled with soy sauce, sugar, and sake.

kimono (kee-mohn-oh)—a long, flowing robe worn by the Japanese people up until the late 19th century. At that time they changed to western style clothing, but, today, kimonos are still used as ceremonial dress on special days on the Japanese calendar.

Hina Matsuri (Hee-na-matsree)—a favorite festival for little girls when a special set of dolls are put on display in their homes each year on March 3rd.